In the Garden of Poisonous Flowers

In the Garden of Poisonous Flowers

Caitlín R. Kiernan

Subterranean Press • 2002

In the Garden of Poisonous Flowers
Copyright © 2002 by Caitlín R. Kiernan
All rights reserved.

Illustrations Copyright © 2002 by Dame Darcy.
All rights reserved.

Limited Edition
(ISBN 1-931081-49-2)

Trade Edition
(ISBN 1-931081-48-4)

Subterranean Press
P.O. Box 190106
Burton, MI 48519

email:
publisher@subterraneanpress.com

website:
www.subterraneanpress.com

author's website:
www.caitlin-r-kiernan.com

*For Dame Darcy
and
Kathryn 'Spooky' Pollnac*

Miles past a town named Vidalia, town named after an onion, onion named after a town, but Dead Girl has no idea how many miles, the vast, unremarkable Georgia night like a seamless quilt of stars and kudzu vines and all these roads look the same to her. The Bailiff behind the wheel of the rustyblack Monte Carlo they picked up in Jacksonville after the Oldsmobile broke down, Bobby in the front seat beside him, playing with the dials on the radio; the endless chain of honky-tonk and gospel stations is broken only by the spit and crackle of static squeezed in between. Dead Girl's alone in the backseat reading one of her books by moonlight. She asks Bobby to stop, please, because he's getting on her nerves, probably getting on The Bailiff's nerves, too. He pauses long enough to glance back at her, and his silver eyes flash like mercury and rainwater coins. He might be any six-year-old boy, except for those eyes.

"Let him be," The Bailiff says. "He isn't bothering me." Bobby smirks at her, sticks out his tongue, and goes back to playing with the radio.

"Suit yourself," and Dead Girl turns a page, even though she hasn't finished reading the last one, tired of looking at it, anyway.

"Well, well, now," The Bailiff says and he laughs his husky, drywheeze laugh. "*There's* a sight."

And the Monte Carlo's brakes squeal, metal grinding metal, and the car drifts off the road. Dead Girl sits up and she can see the hitchhiker in the headlights, a teenage girl holding up one hand to shield her eyes from the glare.

"I'm not hungry," Bobby says as if someone had asked and Dead Girl stares at The Bailiff's reflection in the rearview mirror. But there's no explanation waiting for her in his green eyes, his easy smile, the secretive, parchment creases of his ancient face; she wishes for the hundredth time that she'd stayed in Providence with Gable, better things to do than riding around the sticks picking up runaways and bums. Having to sleep in the trunks of rattletrap automobiles while The Bailiff runs his errands beneath the blazing Southern sun, sun so bright and violent that even the night seems scorched.

"Maybe this one ain't for eating, boy," The Bailiff chuckles and the Monte Carlo rolls to a stop in a cloud of dust and grit and carbon monoxide. "Maybe this one's something you've never seen before."

The girl's wearing dark, wraparound sunglasses and her hair is as white as milk, milk spun into the finest silken thread, talcum powder skin, and "It's just an albino," Dead Girl mutters, disappointed. "You think we've never seen an albino before?"

The Bailiff laughs again and honks the horn. The girl leans forward and squints at them through her sunglasses and the settling dust, takes a hesitant step towards the car. She's wearing a faded yellow Minnie Mouse T-shirt and carrying a tattered duffel bag.

"Pure as the driven snow, this one here. Funeral lilies and barbed wire. Keep your eyes open, both of you, or she just might teach you something you don't *want* to learn."

"Christ," Dead Girl hisses and slumps back in her seat. "I thought we were in such a big, damn hurry. I thought Miss Aramat was—"

"Watch your tongue, child," The Bailiff growls back and now his eyes flash angry emerald fire at her from the rearview mirror. "Mind your *place*," and then Bobby's rolling down his window and the albino girl peers doubtfully into the Monte Carlo.

"Where you bound, sister?" The Bailiff asks and she doesn't answer right away, looks warily at Bobby and Dead Girl and then back at the road stretching away into the summer night.

"Savannah," the albino girl says, finally. "I'm on my way to Savannah," and Dead Girl can hear the misgiving, the guarded apprehension, weighting the edges of her voice.

"Well, now, how about that. Would you believe we're headed that way ourselves? Don't just sit there, Bobby. Open the door for the girl and help her with that bag—"

"Maybe I should wait on the next car," she says and wrinkles her nose like a rabbit. "There's already three of you. There might not be enough room."

"Nonsense," The Bailiff replies. "There's plenty of room, isn't there, chil-

dren?" Bobby opens his door and takes her duffel bag, stuffs it into the floorboard behind his seat. The albino looks at the road one more time and for a moment Dead Girl thinks maybe she's going to run, wonders if The Bailiff will chase her if she does, if it's *that* sort of lesson.

"Thanks," she says, sounding anything but grateful, and climbs into the back and sits beside Dead Girl. Bobby slams his door shut and the Monte Carlo's tires spin uselessly for a moment, flinging up sand and gravel, before they find traction and the car lurches forward onto the road.

"You from Vidalia?" The Bailiff asks and the girl nods her head, but doesn't say anything. Dead Girl closes her book — *Charlotte's Web* in Latin, *Tela Charlottae* — and lays it on the seat between them. The albino smells like old sweat and dirty clothes, like fresh air and the warm blood in her veins. Bobby turns around in his seat and watches her with curious, silver eyes.

"What's her name?" he asks Dead Girl and The Bailiff swerves to miss something lying in the road.

"Dancy," the albino says, "Dancy Flammarion," and she takes off her sunglasses, reveals eyes the deep redpink of pyrope or the pulpy hearts of fresh strawberries.

"Is she blind?" Bobby asks and "How the hell would I know?" Dead Girl grumbles. "Ask her yourself."

"Are you blind?"

"No," Dancy tells him, the hard edge in her voice to say she knows this is a game, a taunting formality, and maybe she's seen it all before. "But the light hurts my eyes."

"Mine, too," Bobby says.

"Oculocutaneous albinism," The Bailiff chimes in. "A genetic defect in the body's ability to convert the amino acid tyrosine into melanin. Ah, but we're being rude, Bobby. She probably doesn't like to talk about it."

"No, that's all right. It doesn't bother me," and Dancy leans suddenly, boldly, forward, leaves only inches between herself and Bobby. The movement surprises him and he jumps.

"What about *you*, Bobby? What's wrong with *your* eyes?"

"I—" he begins and then pauses and looks uncertainly at Dead Girl and The Bailiff. Dead Girl shrugs, no idea what the rules in this charade might be, and The Bailiff keeps his eyes on the road.

"That's okay," Dancy says and she winks at him. "You don't have to tell me if you don't want to, if you're not supposed to tell. The angel tells me what I need to know."

"*You* have an angel?" and now Bobby sounds skeptical.

"Everyone has an angel. Well, everyone I ever met so far. Even you, Bobby. Didn't they tell you that?"

Dead Girl sighs and picks her book up again, opens it to a page she's read twice already.

"Why don't you see if you can find something on the radio," she says to Bobby.

"But I'm still talking to Dancy."

"You'll have plenty of time to talk to Dancy, boy," The Bailiff says. "She isn't going anywhere."

"She's going to Savannah with us."

"Except Savannah," Dancy says very softly, faint smile at the corners of her mouth, and she turns away and looks out the window at the nightshrouded fields and farmhouses rushing silently past. Bobby stares at her for another minute or two, like he's afraid she might disappear, then he goes back to playing with the radio knobs.

"You too, Mercy Brown," the albino whispers and Dead Girl stops reading and *What? What did you say to me?"*

"I dreamed about you once, Mercy. I dreamed about you sleeping at the bottom of a cold river, crabs tangled in your hair and this boy in your arms." Dancy keeps her eyes on the window as she talks, her voice so cool, so unafraid, like maybe she climbs into cars with demons every goddamn night of the week.

"I dreamed about you and snow. You got an angel, too."

"*You* shut the fuck up," Dead Girl snarls. "That's not my name and I don't care *who* you are, you shut up or—"

"You'll kill me anyway," Dancy says calmly, "so what's the difference?" and up front The Bailiff chuckles to himself. Bobby finds a station playing an old Johnny Cash song, "The Reverend Mr. Black," and he sings along.

⁂

Southeast and the land turns from open prairie and piney woods to salt

marsh and estuaries, confluence of muddy, winding rivers, blackwater piss of the distant Appalachians, the Piedmont hills, and everything between. The Lowcountry, *no fayrer or fytter place,* all cordgrass and wax myrtle, herons and crayfish, and the old city laid out wide and flat where the Savannah River runs finally into the patient, hungry sea. The end of Sherman's March and this swampy gem spared the Yankee torches, saved by gracious women and their soiree seductions, and in 1864 the whole city made a grand Christmas gift to Abraham Lincoln.

The mansion on East Hall Street, Stephens Ward, built seventeen long years later, Reconstruction days and Mr. Theodosius W. Ybanes hired a fashionable architect from Rhode Island to design his eclectic, mismatched palace of masonry and wrought iron, Gothic pilasters and high Italianate balconies. The mansard roof tacked on following a hurricane in 1888 and, after Theodosius' death, the house handed down to his children and grandchildren, great-grandchildren, generations come and gone and, unlike most of Savannah's stately, old homes, this house has never passed from the direct bloodline of its first master.

And, at last, delivered across the decades, a furious, red century and decades more, into the small, slender hands of Miss Aramat Drawdes, great-great-great-granddaughter of a Civil War munitions merchant and unspoken matriarch of the Stephens Ward Tea League and Society of Resurrectionists. The first female descendent of Old Ybanes not to take a husband, her sexual, social, and culinary proclivities entirely too unorthodox to permit even a marriage of convenience, but Miss Aramat keeps her own sort of family in the rambling mansion on East Hall Street. Behind yellowglazed brick walls, azaleas and ivy, windows blinded by heavy drapes, the house keeps its own court, its own world apart from the prosaic customs and concerns of the city.

And from appearances, this particular night in June is nothing special, not like the time they found the transsexual junkie who'd hung herself with baling wire in Forsyth Park, or last October, when Candida had the idea of carving all their jack-o'-lanterns from human and ape skulls and then setting them out on the porches in plain sight. Nothing so unusual or extravagant, only the traditional Saturday night indulgences: the nine ladies of the

League and Society (nine now, but there have been more and less, at other times), assembled in the Yellow Room. Antique velvet wallpaper the pungent color of saffron, and they sit, or stand, or lie outstretched on the Turkish carpet, the cushions strewn about the floor and a couple of threadbare recamiers. Miss Aramat and her eight exquisite sisters, the nine who would be proper ghouls if only they'd been born to better skins than these fallible, ephemeral womanhusks. They paint their lips like open wounds, their eyes like bruises. Their fine dresses are not reproductions, every gown and corset and crinoline vintage Victorian or Edwardian, and never anything later than 1914 because that's the year the world ended, Miss Aramat says.

A lump of sticky, black opium in the tall, octopean hookah and there are bottles of burgundy, pear brandy, chartreuse, and cognac, but tonight Miss Aramat prefers the bitter Spanish absinthe and she watches lazily as Isolde balances a slotted silver trowel on the rim of her glass. A single sugar cube and the girl pours water from a carafe over the trowel, dissolving the sugar, drip, drip, drip, and the liqueur turns the milky green of polished jade.

"Me next," Emily demands from her seat on one of the yellow recamiers and Isolde ignores her, pours herself an absinthe and sits on the floor at Miss Aramat's bare feet. She smirks at Emily, who rolls her blue, exasperated eyes and reaches for the brandy instead.

"Better watch yourself, Isolde," Biancabella warns playfully from her place beneath a Tiffany floor lamp, stained-glass light like shattered sunflowers to spill across her face and shoulders. "One day we're gonna have *your* carcass on the table."

"In your dreams," Isolde snaps back, but she nestles in deeper between Miss Aramat's legs, anyway, takes refuge in the protective cocoon of her stockings and petticoat, the folds of her skirt.

Later, of course, there will be dinner, the mahogany sideboard in the dining room laid out with sweetbreads *des champignon,* boiled terrapin lightly flavored with nutmeg and sherry, yams and okra and red rice, raw oysters, Jerusalem artichokes and a dozen deserts to choose from. Then Alma and Biancabella will play for them, cello and violin until it's time to go down to the basement and the evening's anatomizings.

Madeleine turns another card, the Queen of Cups, and Porcelina frowns, not exactly what she was hoping for, already growing bored with Maddy's dry prognostications; she looks over her left shoulder at Miss Aramat.

"I saw Samuel again this week," she says. "He told me the bottle has started to sing at night, if the moon's bright enough."

Miss Aramat stops running her fingers through Isolde's curly, blonde hair and stares silently at Porcelina for a moment. Another sip of absinthe, sugar and anise on her tongue, and "I thought we had an understanding," she says. "I thought I'd asked you not to mention him ever again, not in my presence, not in this house."

Porcelina glances back down at the Tarot card, pushes her violet-tinted pince-nez farther up the bridge of her nose.

"He says that the Jamaicans are offering him a lot of money for it."

Across the room, Candida stops reading to Mary Rose, closes the copy of *Unaussprechlichen Kulten* and glares at Porcelina. "You may be the youngest," she says. "But that's no excuse for impudence. You were told—"

"But I've *seen* it, with my own eyes I've seen it," and now she doesn't sound so bold, not half so confident as only an instant before. Madeleine is trying to ignore the whole affair, gathers up her deck and shuffles the cards.

"You've seen what he wants you to see. What he *made* you see," Miss Aramat says. "Nothing more. The bottle's a fairy tale, and Samuel and the rest of those old conjurers know damn well that's all it will ever be."

"But what if it isn't? What if just one *half* the things he says are true?"

"Drop it," Candida mutters and opens her book again.

"Yes," Mary Rose says. "We're all sick to death of hearing about Samuel and that goddamn bottle."

But Miss Aramat keeps her bottomless, hazelgreen eyes on Porcelina, takes another small swallow of absinthe. She tangles her fingers in Isolde's hair and pulls her head back sharply, exposing the girl's pale throat to the room; they can all see the scars, the puckered, wormpink slashes between Isolde's pretty chin and her high lace collar.

"Then you go and call him, Porcelina," Miss Aramat says very softly. "Tell him to bring the bottle here, tonight. Tell him I want a demonstration."

Madeleine stops shuffling her cards and Biancabella reaches for the brandy, even though her glass isn't empty.

"Before four o'clock, tell him, but after three. I don't want him or one of his little boys interrupting the formalities."

And when she's absolutely certain that Miss Aramat has finished, when Isolde has finally been allowed to lower her chin and hide the scars, Porcelina stands up and goes alone to the telephone in the hallway.

※

In the basement of the house on East Hall Street there are three marble embalming tables laid end to end beneath a row of fluorescent lights. The lights one of Miss Aramat's few, grudging concessions to modernity, though for a time they worked only by candlelight, and then incandescent bulbs strung above the tables. But her eyes aren't what they used to be, and there was Biancabella's astigmatism to consider, as well. So she bought the fluorescents in a government auction at Travis Field and now every corner of the basement is bathed in stark, white light, clinical light to illuminate the most secret recesses of their subjects.

Moldering red brick walls and here and there the sandy, earthen floor has been covered with sheets of varnished plywood, a makeshift, patchwork walkway so their boots don't get too muddy whenever it rains. An assortment of old cabinets and shelves lines the walls, bookshelves and glass-fronted display cases; at least a thousand stoppered apothecary bottles, specimen jars of various shapes and sizes filled with ethyl alcohol or formalin to preserve the ragged things and bits of things that float inside. Antique microscopes, magnifying lenses, and prosthetic limbs, a human skeleton dangling from a hook screwed into the roof of its yellowed skull, each bone carefully labeled with India ink in Miss Aramat's spidery hand.

Alma's collection of aborted and pathologic fetuses occupies the entire northwest corner of the basement, and another corner has been given over to Mary Rose's obsession with the cranium of *Homo sapiens*. So far, she has fifty-three (including the dozen or so sacrificed for Candida's jack-o'-lanterns), classified as Negroid, Australoid, Mongoloid, and Xanthochroid, according T. H. Huxley's 1870 treatise on the races of man. Opposite the embalming tables is a long, low counter of carved and polished oak — half funereal shrine, half laboratory workbench — where Emily's framed photographs of deceased members of the League and Society, lovingly adorned with personal mementos and bouquets of dried flowers, vie for space with Madeleine's jumble of beakers, test tubes, and bell jars.

Nearer the stairs, a great, black double-doored safe that none of them has ever tried to open, gold filigree and L. H. MILLER SAFE AND IRONWORKS, BALTIMORE, MD. painted on one door just above the brass combination dial. Long ago, before Miss Aramat was born, someone stored a portrait of an elderly woman in a blue dress atop the safe, anonymous, unframed canvas propped against the wall, and the years and constant damp have taken their toll. The painting has several large holes, the handiwork of insects and fungi, and the woman's features have been all but obliterated.

"I've never even *heard* of a Skithian," Isolde says, reaching behind her back to tie the strings of her apron.

"*Scy*thian, dear," Miss Aramat corrects her. "S - C - Y, like 'scythe,' but the C and Y make a short 'i' instead of a long 'i.'"

"Oh," Isolde says and yawns. "Well, I've never heard of *them*, either," and she watches as Biancabella makes the first cut, drawing her scalpel expertly between the small breasts of the woman lying on the middle table. Following the undertaker's original Y-incision, she slices cleanly through the sutures that hold the corpse's torso closed.

"An ancient people who probably originated in Anatolia and Northern Mesopotamia," Biancabella says as she carefully traces the line of stitches. "Their kingdom was conquered by the Iranian Suoromata and by the early sixth century BC they'd mostly become nomads wandering the Kuban, and later the Pontic Steppes—"

Isolde yawns again, louder than before, loud enough to interrupt Biancabella. "You sound like a teacher I had in high school. He always smelled like mentholated cough drops."

"They might have *been* Iranian," Madeleine says. "I know I read that somewhere."

Biancabella sighs and stops cutting the sutures, her blade lingering an inch or so above the dead woman's navel, and she glares up at Madeleine.

"They were *not* Iranian. Haven't you even bothered to read Plinius?" she asks and points the scalpel at Madeleine. "'*Ultra sunt Scytharum populi, Persae illos Sacas in universum applelavere a proxima gente, antiqui Arameos.*'"

"Where the hell is Arameos?" Madeleine asks, cocking one eyebrow suspiciously.

"Northern Mesopotamia."

"Who cares?" Isolde mumbles and Biancabella shakes her head in disgust and goes back to work. "Obviously, some more than others," she says.

Miss Aramat reaches for the half-empty bottle of wine that Mary Rose has left on the table near the corpse's knees. She takes a long swallow of the burgundy, wipes her mouth across the back of her hand, smearing her lipstick slightly. "According to Herodotus, the Scythians disemboweled their dead kings," she says and passes the bottle to Isolde. "Then they stuffed the abdominal cavity with cypress, parsley-seed, frankincense, and anise. Afterwards, the body was sewn shut again and entirely covered with wax."

Biancabella finishes with the sutures, lays aside her scalpel and uses both hands to force open the dead woman's belly. The sweet, caustic smells of embalming fluid and rot, already palpable in the stagnant basement air, seem to rise like steam from the interior of the corpse.

"Of course, we don't have the parsley-*seed*," she says and glances across the table at Porcelina, "because someone's Greek isn't exactly what it ought to be."

"It's close enough," Porcelina says defensively and she points an index finger at the bowl of fresh, chopped parsley lined up with all the other ingredients for the ritual. "I can't imagine that Miss Whomever She Might Be here's going to give a damn one way or another."

Biancabella begins inserting her steel dissection hooks through the stiffened flesh at the edges of the incision, each hook attached to a slender chain fastened securely to the rafters overhead. "Will someone please remind me again why we took this little quim in?"

"Well, she's a damn good fuck," Madeleine says. "At least when she's sober."

"And she makes a mean corn pudding," Alma adds.

"Oh, yes. The corn pudding. How could I have possibly forgotten the corn pudding."

"Next time," Porcelina growls, "you can fucking do it yourselves."

"No, dear," Miss Aramat says, her voice smooth as the tabletop, cold as the heart of the dead woman. "Next time, you'll do it right. Or there may not be another time after that."

Porcelina turns her back on them, then, turning because she's afraid they might see straight through her eyes to the hurt and doubt coiled about her soul. She stares instead at the louvered window above Mary Rose's skulls, the glass painted black, shinythick black latex to stop the day and snooping eyes.

"Well, you have to admit, at least then we'd never have to hear about that fucking bottle again," Candida laughs and, as though her laughter were an incantation, skillful magic to shatter the moment, the back doorbell rings directly overhead. Buzz like angry, electric wasps filtered through the floorboards and Miss Aramat looks at Porcelina, who hasn't taken her eyes off the window.

"You told him three o'clock?" Miss Aramat asks.

"I *told* him," Porcelina replies, sounding scared, and Miss Aramat nods her head once, takes off her apron, and returns it to a bracket on the wall.

"If I need you, I'll call," she says to Biancabella, and, taking what remains of the burgundy, goes upstairs to answer the door.

❧

"Maybe Bobby and me should stay with the car," Dead Girl says again, in case The Bailiff didn't hear her the first time. Big, blustery man fiddling with his keys, searching for the one that fits the padlock on the iron gate; he stops long enough to glance back at her and shake his head no. The moonlight glints dull off his bald head and he scratches at his beard and glares at the uncooperative keys.

"But I saw a cop back there," Dead Girl says. "What if he finds the car and runs the plates? What if—"

"We can always get another car," The Bailiff grumbles. "Better he finds a stolen car than a stolen car with the two of you sitting inside."

"And I wanna see the ladies," Bobby chirps, swings The Bailiff's leather satchel, and Dead Girl wishes she could smack him, would if The Bailiff wasn't standing right there to see her do it.

Bobby leans close to the albino girl and stands on tiptoes, his lips pressed somewhere below her left ear. There's a piece of duct tape across her mouth, silver duct tape wrapped tight around her wrists, and Dead Girl's holding onto the collar of her Minnie Mouse T-shirt. "They're like *ghouls,*" he whispers, "only nicer."

"No, they're not," Dead Girl snorts. "Not real ghouls. Real ghouls don't live in great big fucking houses."

"You'll see," Bobby whispers to Dancy. "They dig up dead people and cut them into pieces. That's what ghouls do."

And The Bailiff finds the right key, then— "*There* you are, my rusty, little sparrow." —and the hasp pops open and in a moment they're through the gate and standing in the garden. Dead Girl looks longingly back at the alleyway and the Monte Carlo as The Bailiff pulls the gate shut behind him, *clang*, and snaps the padlock closed again.

The garden is darker than the alley, the low, sprawling limbs of live oaks and magnolias to hide the moon, crooked limbs draped with Spanish moss and epiphytic ferns. Dancy has to squint to see. She draws a deep breath through her nostrils, taking in the sticky, flowerscented night, camellias and boxwood, the fleshy, white magnolia blossoms. Behind her, The Bailiff's keys jangle and Dead Girl shoves her roughly forward, towards the house.

The Bailiff leads the way down the narrow, cobblestone path that winds between the trees, past a brass sundial and marble statues set on marble pedestals, nude bodies wrapped in shadow garments, unseeing stone eyes staring after Heaven. Dancy counts her steps, listens to The Bailiff's fat-man wheeze, the twin silences where Dead Girl and Bobby's breath should be. Only the slightest warm breeze to disturb the leaves, the drone of crickets and katydids, and somewhere nearby a whippoorwill calling out to other whippoorwills.

A thick hedge of oleander bushes and then the path turns abruptly and they're standing at the edge of a reflecting pool

choked with hyacinth and water lilies; broad flagstones to ring its dark circumference and The Bailiff pauses here, stares down at the water and rubs his beard. The expression on his face like someone who's lost something, someone who knows he'll never find it again, or it'll never find him.

"What is it?" Dead Girl asks. "What's wrong?" but The Bailiff only shrugs his broad shoulders, and takes another step nearer the pool, standing right at the very edge now.

"One day," he says. "One day when you're older, maybe, I'll tell you about this place. One day maybe I'll even tell you what she keeps trapped down there at the bottom with the goldfish and the tadpoles."

He laughs, an ugly, bitter sound, and Dancy makes herself turn away from the pool. She can hear the drowned things muttering to themselves below the surface, even if Dead Girl can't, the rheumy voices twined with roots and slime. She looks up at the house instead and sees they've almost reached the steps leading to the high back porch. Some of the downstairs windows glow with soft, yellow light, light that can't help but seem inviting after so much darkness. But Dancy knows better, knows a lie when she sees one and there's nothing to comfort or save her behind those walls. She takes another deep breath and starts walking towards the steps before Dead Girl decides to shove her again.

"You still got that satchel?" The Bailiff asks and "Yes sir," the boy with silver eyes answers and holds it up so he can see. "It's getting heavy."

"Well, you just hang in there, boy. It's going to be getting a whole lot lighter any minute now."

And they climb the stairs together, Dancy in the lead, still counting the paces, The Bailiff at the rear, and the wooden steps creak loud beneath their feet. At the top, The Bailiff presses the doorbell and Dead Girl pushes Dancy into an old wicker chair.

"Where's your angel now?" she sneers and digs her sharp nails into the back of Dancy's neck, forces her head down between her knees.

"Be careful, child," The Bailiff says. "Don't start asking questions you don't really want answered," and now he's staring back towards the alley, across the wide, wide garden towards the car. "She might show you an angel or two, before this night's done."

And Dead Girl opens her mouth to tell him to fuck off and never mind her "place" because baby-sitting crazy albino girls was never part of the deal. But the back door opens then, light spilling from the house and Dead Girl and Bobby both cover their eyes and look away. Dancy raises her head, wishing they hadn't taken her sunglasses, and she strains to see more than the silhouette of the woman standing in the doorway.

"Well, isn't this a surprise," the woman says and then she leads them all inside.

※

Through the bright kitchen and down a long, dimly lit hall, walls hung with gilt-framed paintings of worse things even than Dancy's nightmares, worse things than she's seen so far. Cemetery pictures, opened graves, broken headstones, and the hunched and prancing figures, dogjawed, fire-eyed, dragging corpses from the violated earth.

"We can have our tea in the Crimson Room," the woman named Miss Aramat says to The Bailiff. Small woman barely as tall as Dancy, china-doll hands and face, china-doll clothes, and Dancy thinks she might shatter if she fell, if anyone ever struck her. The jewels about her throat sparkle like drops of blood and morning dew set in silver, and she's wearing a big, black hat, broad-brimmed and tied with bunches of lace and ribbon, two iridescent peacock feathers stuck in the band. Her waist cinched so small that Dancy imagines one hand would reach almost all the way around it, thumb to middle finger. She isn't old, though Dancy wouldn't exactly call her a young woman, either.

Miss Aramat opens a door and ushers them into a room the color of a slaughterhouse: red walls, red floors, crossed swords above a red-tiled fireplace, a stuffed black bear wearing a red fez standing guard in one corner. She tugs on a braided bell-pull and somewhere deep inside the house there's the muffled sound of chimes.

"I didn't expect you until tomorrow night," she says to The Bailiff and motions for him to take a seat in an armchair upholstered with cranberry brocade.

"Jacksonville took less time than I'd expected," he replies, shifting his weight about, trying to find a comfortable way to

sit in an uncomfortable chair. "You seemed anxious to get this shipment. I trust we're not intruding—"

"Oh, no, no," Miss Aramat says. "Of course not," and she smiles a smile that makes Dancy think of an alligator.

"Well, this time I have almost everything you asked for," and the armchair cracks loudly and he stops fidgeting and sits still, glances apologetically at Miss Aramat. "Except the book. I'm afraid my man on Magazine Street didn't come through on that count."

"Ah. I'm sorry to hear that. Biancabella will be disappointed."

"However," The Bailiff says quickly and jabs a pudgy thumb towards Dancy, who's sitting now between Dead Girl and Bobby on a long, red sofa. "I think perhaps I have something here that's going to more than make up for it."

And Miss Aramat pretends she hasn't already noticed Dancy, that she hasn't been staring at her for the last five minutes. "That's marvelous," she says, though Dancy catches the doubtful edge in her voice, the hesitation. "I don't think we've ever had an albino before."

"Oh, she's not just any albino," The Bailiff says, grins and scratches his beard.

"You must have heard about the unpleasantness in Waycross last month. Well, *this* is the girl who did the killing."

And something passes swiftly across Miss Aramat's face, then, fleeting wash of fear or indignation, and she takes a step back towards the doorway.

"My god, man. And you brought her *here?*"

"Don't worry. I think she's actually quite harmless."

The Bailiff winks at Dead Girl and she slams an elbow into Dancy's ribs to prove his point. Her breath rushes out through her nostrils and she doubles over, gasping uselessly against the duct tape still covering her mouth. A sickening swirl of black and purple fireflies dances before her eyes, and *I'm going to throw up*, she thinks. *I'm going throw up and choke to death*.

"You ask me, someone must be getting sloppy down there in Waycross," The Bailiff says, "if this skinny little bitch could do that much damage. Anyway, when we found her, I thought to myself, now who would appreciate such an extraordinary morsel as this, such a tender, pink delicacy."

Miss Aramat is chewing indecisively at a thumbnail and she tugs the bell-pull again, harder this time, impatient, stomps the floor twice, and "No extra charge?" she asks.

"Not a penny. You'll be doing us all a favor."

Dancy shuts her eyes tight, breathing through her nose, tasting blood and bile at the back of her mouth. The Bailiff and Miss Aramat are still talking, but their voices seem far away now, inconsequential. This is the house where she's going to die and she doesn't understand why the angels never told her that. The night in Waycross when she drove her knife into the heart of a monster dressed in the skin of a girl who was never born, or before that, the one she killed in Bainbridge. Each time the angels there to tell her it was right, the world a cleaner place for her work, but never a word about this house and the woman in the wide, peacock hat. Slowly, the dizziness and nausea begin to pass even if the pain doesn't, and she opens her eyes again and stares at the antique rug between her tennis shoes.

"I said *look* at me," and it takes Dancy a moment to realize that the woman's talking to her. She turns her head, and now Miss Aramat's standing much closer than before and there are two younger women standing on either side of her.

"*She* killed the Gynander?" the very tall woman on Miss Aramat's right asks skeptically. "Jesus," and she wipes her hands on the black rubber apron she's wearing, adjusts her spectacles for a better view.

The auburn-haired woman on Miss Aramat's left shakes her head, disbelieving or simply amazed. "What do you think she'd taste like, Biancabella? I have a Brazilian recipe for veal I've never tried—"

"Oh, no. We're not wasting this one in the stew pot."

"I'll have to get plantains, of course. And lots of fresh lime."

"Aramat, tell her this one's for the slab. Anyway, she looks awfully stringy."

"Yes, but I can marinate—"

"Just bring the tea, Alma," Miss Aramat says, interrupting the auburn-haired woman. "And sweets for the boy. I think there are still some blueberry tarts left from breakfast. You may call Isolde up to help you."

"But you're not really going to let Biancabella have *all* of her, are you?"

"We'll talk about it later. Get the tea. The jasmine, please."

And Alma sulks away towards the kitchen, mumbling to herself; Biancabella watches her go. "It's a wonder she's not fat as a pig," she says.

Miss Aramat kneels in front of Dancy, brushes cornsilk bangs from her white-rabbit eyes, and when Dancy tries to pull back, Dead Girl grabs a handful of her hair and holds her still.

"Does she bite?" Miss Aramat asks Dead Girl, points at the duct tape, and Dead Girl shrugs.

"She hasn't bitten me. I just got tired of listening to her talk about her goddamn angels."

"Angels?"

"She has an angel," Bobby says. "She says everyone has an angel, even me. Even Dead Girl."

"Does she really?" Miss Aramat asks the boy, most of her apprehension gone and something like delight creeping into her voice to fill the void.

"Her angel tells her where to find monsters and how to kill them."

"Angels and monsters," Miss Aramat whispers and she smiles, her fingertips gently stroking Dancy's cheeks, skin so pale it's almost translucent. "You must be a regular Joan of Arc, then, *la pucelle de Dieu* to send us all scuttling back to Hell."

"She's a regular *nut*," Dead Girl says and draws circles in the air around her right ear.

The Bailiff laughs and the armchair cracks again.

"Is that true, child? Are you insane?" and Miss Aramat pulls the duct tape slowly off Dancy's mouth, drops it to the carpet. It leaves behind an angry red swatch of flesh, perfect rectangle to frame her lips, and Miss Aramat leans forward and kisses her softly. Dancy stiffens, but Dead Girl's hand there to keep her from pulling away. Only a moment, and when their mouths part, there's a faint smear of rouge left behind on Dancy's lips.

"Strange," Miss Aramat says, touching the tip of her tongue to her front teeth. "She tastes like hemlock."

"She *smells* like shit," Dead Girl sneers and yanks hard on Dancy's hair.

Miss Aramat ignores Dead Girl, doesn't take her eyes off Dancy's face.

"Do you know, child, what it meant a hundred years ago, when a man sent a woman a bouquet of hemlock? It meant,

'You will be my death.' But no, you didn't know that, did you?"

Dancy closes her eyes, remembering all the times that have been so much worse than this, all the horror and shame and sorrow to give her strength. The burning parts of her no one and nothing can ever touch, the fire where her soul used to be.

"Look at me when I talk to you," Miss Aramat says and Dancy does, opens her eyes wide and spits in the woman's china-doll face.

"Whore." Dancy screams, and "*Witch,*" before Dead Girl clamps a hand over her mouth.

"Guess you should've left the tape on after all," she snickers and Miss Aramat takes a deep breath, fishes a lace handkerchief from the cuff of one sleeve and wipes away the spittle clinging to her face. She stares silently at the damp linen for a moment while Dead Girl laughs and The Bailiff mumbles half-hearted apologies behind her.

"A needle and thread will do a better job, I think," Miss Aramat says calmly and gets up off her knees. She passes the handkerchief to Biancabella and then makes a show of smoothing the wrinkles from her dress.

Then Alma comes back with a silver serving tray, cups and saucers, cream and sugar, a teapot trimmed in gold and there are violets painted on the side. Porcelina's a step behind her, carrying another, smaller silver tray piled with cakes and tarts and a bowl of chocolate bonbons.

"We were out of jasmine," Alma says. "So I used the rose hip and chamomile instead."

"What's she doing up here?" and Miss Aramat points at Porcelina. "I told you to call for Isolde."

Alma frowns, sets the tray down on a walnut table near The Bailiff, and "I did," she says. "But Porcelina came."

"Isolde was busy draining the corpse," Porcelina explains and she puts her tray down beside the other. "And I've never seen vampires before."

"Is it everything you always hoped it would be?" Dead Girl purls.

"Rose hip and chamomile sounds just wonderful," The Bailiff says, taking a saucer and two sugar cubes. "And are those poppy-seed cakes?"

Miss Aramat stares at Porcelina, who pretends not to notice, while Alma pours steaming tea into the cups.

"Yes, they are," Porcelina says. "Mary Rose baked them just this morning."

"Delightful. I haven't had a good poppy-seed cake in ages."

"Can I please have two of these?" Bobby asks, poking the sticky, indigo filling of a blueberry tart lightly dusted with confectioner's sugar.

"I don't see why not, dear. They'll only go to waste otherwise."

And the sudden, swelling howl from Miss Aramat, rabid sound much too big, too wild, to ever have fit inside her body, her narrow throat, but it spills out, anyway. She turns and rushes towards the red fireplace, stretching up on tiptoes to snatch one of the swords from its bracket above the mantel. Broadsword almost as long as she is tall, but such grace in her movement, the silver arc of tempered steel, that it might weigh no more than a broomstick.

Alma shrieks and drops the violet-dappled teapot and the cup she was filling. They seem to fall forever as the sword swings round like the needle of some deadly compass, finally smashing wetly against the floor in the same instant that the blade comes to rest beneath Porcelina's chin. The razor point pressed to the soft place beneath her jawbone, only a little more pressure and she'd bleed, a thrust and the blade would slide smoothly through windpipe cartilage and into her spine.

The Bailiff stops chewing, his mouth stuffed with poppy-seed cake, the sword only inches from the end of his nose. He reaches slowly for the automatic pistol tucked into the waistband of his trousers, and Bobby turns and runs back to Dead Girl.

The grin on Miss Aramat's face like rictus, wide and toothy corpsegrin and "Biancabella," she says, but the fury has drained out of her, leaving her voice barely a hoarse murmur. "Remember last winter, when you wanted to do *Salomé?* Maybe our guests would enjoy the entertainment—"

"She'll make a poor Jokanaan," Biancabella says, her eyes on The Bailiff's hand as he flips off the gun's safety and aims the barrel at Miss Aramat's head.

"Oh, *I* think she'll do just fine," and now the point of the sword draws a single, scarlet bead from Porcelina's throat.

"*Please.* I'm sorry. I only wanted to see—"

"'She is monstrous, thy daughter, she is altogether monstrous. In truth, what she

has done is a *great* crime.'"

The Bailiff swallows and licks his lips, catching the last stray crumbs. "You're very thoughtful, Aramat," he says coolly, politely, as if declining another cake or another cup of tea. "Some other time, perhaps."

"'I will not *look* at things, I will not suffer things to look at *me*—'"

"For fuck's sake," Biancabella hisses. "You know that he means it."

Aramat glances sidewise at The Bailiff and his gun, and then quickly back to Porcelina. Her grin slackens to a wistful, sour sort of smile, and she lowers the blade until the point is resting on the tea-stained carpet.

"I didn't want you thinking I wasn't a good host," she says, her eyes still fixed on Porcelina. The girl hasn't moved, stands trembling like a palsied statue; a thin trickle of blood is winding its way towards the collar of her dress.

"You understand that, Bailiff. I couldn't have you going back up to Providence and Boston, telling them all I wasn't a good host."

The Bailiff breathes out stale air and relief, and slowly he lowers his gun, easing his finger off the trigger.

"Now, you know I'd never say a thing like that, Miss Aramat." And he puts the gun away and reaches for one of the cups of tea. "I *always* look forward to our visits."

"I really wasn't expecting you until tomorrow night," she says, and Biancabella takes the sword from her hands, returns it to its place above the mantle. Miss Aramat thanks her and sits down in a salon chair near The Bailiff, but she doesn't take her eyes off Porcelina until Alma has led her from the room.

On the red sofa, Dancy turns her head and looks at Dead Girl and the frightened boy in her arms. Empty, silver eyes in ageless, unaging faces. Eyes that might have seen hundreds of years or only decades and it really makes no difference, one way or the other, when a single moment can poison a soul forever. "Can I please have something to drink," she asks and Dead Girl whispers in Bobby's ear. He nods his head, takes his arms from around her neck, and sits silently on the sofa next to Dancy while Dead Girl goes to get her a cup of tea.

※

Sometime later, though Dancy can't be sure how much later, no clocks in the red room, but an hour, surely, since they left her alone on the sofa. The contents of the leather satchel traded for a fat roll of bills and The Bailiff turned and winked at her before he left. Miss Aramat and Biancabella followed him and Dead Girl and Bobby back out into the hall, shutting and locking the door behind them. There's only one small window, set high up on the wall past the fireplace, but if her hands weren't still strapped together with duct tape maybe she could reach it, if she stood on one of the chairs or tables.

"They'd only catch you," the black bear in the corner says. "They'd catch you and bring you right back again." It hadn't surprised her very much when the bear had started talking to her in his gruff, sawdusty, stuffed-bear voice.

"They might not," she says. "I can run fast."

"They can run faster," the bear says, unhelpfully.

Dancy stares at the bear, at the ridiculous hat perched between his ears. She'd asked him if he could talk to anyone or just to her, because sometimes there were things that could only talk to her, things only she could hear because no one else would ever listen. "I talked to the man who shot me," the bear growled. "And I spoke to Candida once, but she told me she'd throw me out with the trash if I ever did it again."

"What will they do to me?" Dancy asks and when the bear doesn't answer her, she asks again. "What are they going to do to me, bear?"

"I'd rather not say."

"Stupid bear. You probably don't have any idea what goes on in this house."

The bear grumbles to itself and stares straight ahead with its glass eyeballs. "I wish I didn't," he says. "I wish the taxidermist had forgotten to give me eyes to see or ears to hear. I wish the hunter had left me to rot in the woods."

"They're very wicked women," Dancy says, watching the door now instead of the bear. He doesn't reply, tired of listening to her or maybe he's gone back to sleep, whatever it is dead bears do instead of sleep. She gets up and crosses the room, stands in front of two paintings hung side by side above a potted plant. Both are portraits of dead women.

"Is this a riddle?" she asks the bear.

"I don't answer riddles," the bear replies.

"That's not what I asked you."

"If I still had a stomach," the bear says. "I'd like one of those chocolate bonbons there," and then he doesn't point at the silver serving platter because he can't move, and Dancy decides she's better off ignoring him and looks at the two paintings instead.

The one on the right shows a naked corpse so emaciated that she can make out the sharp jut of its hip bones, the peaks and valleys of its ribs. Sunken, hollow eyes, gaping mouth, and the woman's left breast has sagged so far that it's settled in her armpit. She lies on a bare slab and there's only a hard, wooden block to prop up her skull.

"You could put one into my mouth. I might remember how to taste it."

"Shut up, bear," and now Dancy examines the painting on her left. This dead woman might only be sleeping, if not for the grief on the face of the old man seated there at her side. Her hands folded neatly across her breasts, and she's dressed in a satin gown and lies on a bed covered with white roses, two soft pillows tucked beneath her head.

"It *is* a riddle," Dancy says. "One is the truth and one isn't. Or they're both true, but only partly true. They're both lies, without the other."

"Give me a bonbon and I'll tell you which," the stuffed bear growls.

"You don't answer riddles. You said so."

"I'll make an exception."

"I don't think you even know."

"I'm dead. Dead bears know lots of things," and Dancy's thinking about that, trying to decide whether or not she could even get a piece of the candy all the way up into the bear's mouth with her wrists tied together. "All right," she says, but then there's a rustling sound behind her, like dry October leaves in a cold breeze, and the air smells suddenly of cinnamon and ice.

I never knew ice had a smell, she thinks, turning and there's a very pretty boy standing on the other side of the room, watching her. The door's still closed, or he shut it again. He's tall and very slender, maybe a little older than she is, and

wearing a black velvet dress with a dark green symbol like an hourglass embroidered over his flat chest. His long hair is the exact same green as the hourglass, and his eyes are the color of starlight.

"Hello, Dancy," he says, and takes a step towards her. He's barefoot and has a silver ring on each of his toes. "Who were you talking to?"

"The bear," she says and the boy smiles and reaches into a pocket of his skirt; he takes out a small, stoppered bottle and holds it up where she can see. The glass is the amber color of pine sap or deep, swamp pools stained by rotting vegetation.

"The Ladies have asked me to speak to you," he tells her. "I've brought them something quite precious, but they thought you should see it first. And, I admit, I've been wanting to see you for myself. You have a lot of people talking, Dancy Flammarion."

"Did you know he was coming?" she asks the bear, or her angel, it doesn't really matter which, since neither of them answer her.

"You're not exactly what any of us expected. Why did you come to Savannah? Who did you come here to kill?"

"I'm not sure," she says, and that much the truth, all her dreams after Waycross, all the things she sees in dark hours, only bits and tattered pieces, something broken and there wasn't time to figure out how all the parts fit together.

"You didn't come for The Ladies?"

"They're not real monsters," she says. "They're nothing but witches and perverts and cannibals. They're all crazy, but they're not real monsters at all."

"No," he says. "They're not. Did you come for me, then? Did you come for my master or one of The Parsifal?"

"I don't know."

"Did you come for this?" and the boy in the black dress holds the bottle out to her and Dancy looks back at the bear again, imagines a story where it springs suddenly to life and leaps across the room to devour this strange boy in a single bite.

"No. I don't even know what that is," she says.

For a moment, the boy doesn't say anything else, watches her with his brilliant, starshine eyes, eyes to read her mind, her soul, to ferret out lies and half truths. They're starting to make her feel light-headed, those eyes, and she glances down at the floor.

"Do I frighten you, Dancy?"

"No," she lies. "I'm not scared of you."

"Look at me then," he says and when she does, Dancy sees that she isn't standing by the bear and the dead-woman paintings anymore, but sitting on the red sofa again, and the duct tape binding her hands is gone. The pretty boy is sitting beside her, on her left, staring down at the amber bottle in his hand. The glass looks very old, oily, iridescent. He shakes it and inside something buzzes and flickers to life, lightning-bug flicker, and soon the bottle has begun to glow as brightly as the fancy lamps set around the room and she can't look directly at it anymore.

"Some people still think that it's The Grail," he says. "It isn't, of course. The alchemist Petrus Bonus thought it might be a splinter of the *lapis exilis*, but it isn't that, either. For a long time, it was lost. It turned up a few years ago in a Portuguese fisherman's nets, trapped inside this bottle. The fisherman died trying to open it."

"So what is it?" Dancy asks, trying not to hear the low, thrumming voices woven into the light from the bottle. A rumbling, thunderstorm choir to rattle her teeth, to make ashes of her bones and soot of her white flesh.

"Just a toy. An unfinished experiment. Some forgotten, second-rate wizard's silly trinket."

"Then it isn't precious at all," Dancy says and her eyes have started to hurt so badly that she looks away. Tears are streaming down her cheeks and the thrumming sound is starting to make her head ache.

"It's quite useless, but there are people who would die for it. There are people who would kill for it."

"You're just another riddle, aren't you?" Dancy whispers. "I'm sick of riddles." She's holding her fingertips to her temples, eyes squeezed shut, the voices stuck inside her head now and trying to force their way out through her skull.

"But that's all there is, I'm afraid. In the whole, wide, irredeemable world, that's all there is, finally."

"No. That's not true," Dancy says. "There's pain—"

"But why? *Why* is there pain, Dancy?"

"So there can be an end to pain," and she wishes on the names of all the saints and angels she can remember that the boy

will stop talking, stop asking her questions, kill her and get it over with. She doesn't want to be alive when the voices from the bottle find their way out of her head.

"What do you hear, Dancy Flammarion? The voices, what do they sing for you? What songs do they sing for martyrs and monster slayers?"

"They *hate* you," she says and then bites down hard on the end of her tongue so that she won't say anything else, nothing else she isn't supposed to say. Her mouth tastes like salt and wheat pennies and rainwater.

"That's nothing I didn't already know. What do they sing for my oblation, for your sacrifice?"

The throb behind her eyes folding and unfolding, becoming something unbearable, unthinkable, that stretches itself across the sizzling sky, running on forever or so far it may as well be forever. A choir of agony, razorshard crescendo, and "Haven't you ever tried to open the bottle?" Dancy asks the boy because she can't keep it all inside herself any longer.

And for her answer, the rustling, autumn sound again, though this time she thinks it's actually more like wings, leathery bat wings or the nervous wings of small birds, the flutter of ten thousand flapping wings, and Dancy knows that if she opens her eyes it won't be the boy sitting next to her. Something else entirely, something much closer to whatever he really is, and now the red room stinks of roadkill and shit and garbage left to slowly rot beneath the summer sun.

"It's only a toy," she says.

"That's what he's afraid of," the stuffed bear growls from across the room and Dancy laughs, because she knows he's telling the truth. Dead bears don't like riddles, either, and when she tries to stand up she falls, tumbles like a dropped teapot that would never stop falling if she had a choice, would never have to shatter like the china-doll woman who shattered a long, long time ago and the Savannah River washed most of the pieces away to the sea.

Dancy opens her eyes and the bottle's lying on the floor in front of her. The roaring, hurtful voices inside drip from her nostrils and lips and ears, a stickydark, molasses puddle on the rug and "Pick it up," the thing that isn't a boy in a dress snarls, making words from the tumult of feathers and hurricane wind. "You're dying, anyway. There's nothing it can do to you. Show me the trick."

"There *isn't* any trick," she says, reaching for the bottle. "It's only a toy."

"No," the bear growls. "Don't you touch it. Make him do his own dirty work," but she's already holding the bottle, so light in her hand, so warm, a balm to soothe the pain eating her alive, and she looks up into the maelstrom spinning in the bruised place hung a few feet above the red sofa. The counterclockwise gyre of snapping, twigthin bones and mockingbird quills, the eyes like swollen, seeping wounds, and *here,* this part she remembers, this moment from a nightmare of hungry, whirling fire and dying birds.

"You should have tried the window," the bear says and Dancy vomits, nothing much in her stomach but the tea that Dead Girl let her drink, but she vomits anyway.

"It *knows* you, Dancy Flammarion. Before you were born, it knew you. Before the sun sparked to life, it was *already* calling you here."

"I don't want it," she coughs and wipes her mouth.

"*You* know *the trick. We* know *you know the trick,*" and the thing in the air above the sofa is screaming, screeching, turning faster and faster, and bits of itself are coming loose and drifting slowly down to the floor. Wherever they land, the rug scorches and smolders.

"*Open it!*"

Dancy sits up and for a moment she stares deep into the wheel, the paradox still point at its absolute center — consuming and blossoming heart, nothing and everything there all at once. "Abracadabra," she whispers, her throat gone raw and her head coming apart at the seams, and she throws the bottle as hard as she can. It arcs end over end and the pretty boy with starshine eyes (and she sees that he *has* become a boy again, that the boy was there somewhere, all along) is scrambling after it. When the bottle hits the wall it bursts into a spray of powdered glass and bluegolden flame that rises quickly towards the ceiling. A sparkling ruin that twines itself into a hammer, a wave, a fist of the purest light, and as the pain leaves her head and the world slips kindly away to leave her alone in darkness, the hammer falls and the only sounds left are the promises that monsters make before they die.

❦

"Is it over?" Mary Rose asks, speaking very quietly, and Biancabella holds an index finger up to her lips, hush.

The ladies of the Stephens Ward Tea League and Society of Resurrectionists wait together in the long hall outside the door to the Crimson Room. Miss Aramat is sitting on the stairs, alone with Porcelina's body in her arms, singing softly to herself or to Porcelina's ghost, *Blacks and bays, dapples and grays, when you wake you shall have all the pretty little horses*. The kitchen knife she used to cut Porcelina's throat lies at her feet, sticky with drying blood. The house on East Hall Street is quiet now, breathless in the battered silence after the storm, and there's only Miss Aramat's voice and the obstinate ticking of the grandfather clock by the stairs, the distant ticking of other clocks in other rooms.

All the things they've heard, or only think they've heard, since The Bailiff left and Samuel's boy went into the room with his bottle and the albino girl, the inescapable, inevitable moment of Porcelina's death, but all of it not half so terrible as this silence. This waiting, and once Candida put her hand on the doorknob and pulled it quickly back again, her palm scalded raw by the cold.

"He used us," Isolde murmurs. "He *lied* to us," and "They *both* used us," Emily replies, then the look from Miss Aramat enough that neither of them says anything more.

Just the clocks and pretty little horses and the long, last hour before dawn.

And then the knob turns, finally, the tumblers of the lock rolling themselves, the irrelevant key in Biancabella's pocket, and the door swings open. Dancy Flammarion stands silhouetted in lamplight and a weirder, flaxen glow, fairy fire, foxfire, that seems to shine from somewhere just behind her. A power in that light, and dignity, and darker things that will haunt the dreams of The Ladies for the rest of their lives. But the glow fades immediately away when she steps out into the shadow-strewn hallway, and she's only The Bailiff's hitchhiker again.

Dancy holds one of the swords from over the fireplace gripped tight in both hands. Her face is streaked with tears and blood and vomit, and Biancabella notices that one of her shoes is untied.

Miss Aramat stops singing and "What did you do to him?" she asks. "Is he dead? Did you kill him?"

"He would have let you open the bottle for him," Dancy says. "He would have let you all die trying."

Miss Aramat looks down at Porcelina's head in her lap and she smiles sadly and strokes the dead girl's matted hair.

"What was in it?" she whispers.

"Nothing meant for you. Nothing meant for him, either."

"I tried to tell her," Miss Aramat says, wiping a bloody smear from underneath Porcelina's left eye. "I tried to tell her we wanted nothing to do with the goddamned thing."

"Is that why you killed her?"

Miss Aramat wipes away another splotch of blood and then she closes Porcelina's eyes. "I can't remember why I killed her," she says. "I knew for certain, only a moment ago, but now I can't remember. Do you know, Biancabella?"

"You were angry," Biancabella replies, keeping her eyes on the sword in Dancy's hands. "You were afraid."

"Was I? Well, there you go, then. Biancabella's hardly ever wrong."

"Are you going to kill us all now?" Alma asks. "We wouldn't really have hurt you, you know, not really. We were only—"

"Jesus Christ, Alma," Biancabella says. "You only wanted to cook her with plantains. Shut up or I'll kill you myself."

"I'm leaving now," Dancy says and she takes another step away from the door to the Crimson Room, still holding the sword out in front of her like a shield. Alma and Candida step out of her way and "Thank you, oh thank you," Alma gushes. "We wouldn't have hurt you, not really. We would never, ever—"

"Alma, I *told* you to shut the fuck up!"

"I'm sorry," and Alma's backing away from Dancy and Biancabella both, presses herself insect flat against the wall. "I won't say anything else, I promise. I'm sorry I ever said anything at all."

"Get the hell out of here, girl," Biancabella growls. "*Now*, before I change my mind. I don't give a shit what happened in there, you couldn't kill all of us."

Dancy glances at the sword and then nods once, because she knows that Biancabella's probably right and what she came to do is finished, so it doesn't matter anyway. She turns and hurries towards the front door. Outside, the first watery hints of dawn, grayblue wash through the window set into the little door, and she never thought she'd see daylight again.

"Stop!" Miss Aramat shouts and when she stands up, Porcelina's body rolls forward and tumbles loudly to the bottom of the stairs. *So close,* Dancy thinks, *so close*, only two or three more steps and she would have been out the door and running down the street and she wouldn't have looked back even once.

"It doesn't end this way," Miss Aramat says and when Dancy turns around, the china-doll woman's holding a revolver pointed at her. "Not in my house, missy. You don't come into my house and make threats and then walk out the front door like nothing's happened."

"Let her go," Biancabella says. "It's not worth it."

"We have to have a feast to remember Porcelina by, don't we? We'll have to have something *special,*" and Miss Aramat pulls the trigger. There's a small, hard *click* as the hammer falls on an empty chamber.

"I didn't come for you," Dancy says and she tightens her grip on the sword because it's the only thing left to hold onto.

"You're nothing but a wicked, crazy woman."

"And *you*, you think you're better? You're so goddamn high and mighty, standing there on the side of the goddamn angels, and we're nothing but shit, is that it?"

"Please, Aramat," Biancabella begs. "We'll find something else for Porcelina's feast, something truly special. We'll take the car and drive down to St. Augustine—"

"*Look* at her, Biancabella. *She's* the monster. She has the marks," and Miss Aramat pulls the revolver's trigger again, and again there's only the impotent taunt of the hammer falling on an empty chamber.

"Let her go, Aramat," and now Biancabella's moving towards the stairs. She shoves Isolde roughly aside and almost trips over Porcelina's corpse. "She's *nothing* to us. She's just someone's fucking puppet."

"I didn't come for you," Dancy says again.

"'I *will* kiss thy mouth, Jokanaan,'" Miss Aramat whispers and the third time she squeezes the trigger the revolver explodes in a deafening flash of fire and thunder, tearing itself apart, and the shrapnel takes her hands and face with it, buries a chunk of steel the size of a grape between her eyes. One of the fragments grazes Biancabella's left cheek, digging a bloody furrow from the corner of her mouth to her ear, and she stands, helpless, at the bottom of the stairs as Aramat crumples and falls.

And Dancy Flammarion doesn't wait to see whatever does or doesn't come next. She drops the sword and runs, out the front door of the big house on East Hall Street, across the wide yard, and the new day wraps her safe in redeeming, charcoal wings and hides her steps.

※

Not yet noon and already a hundred degrees in the shade, and The Bailiff is sitting alone on the rusted rear bumper of the Monte Carlo drinking a Coke. The sun a proper demon overhead, and he holds the cool bottle pressed to his forehead for a moment and squints into the mirage shimmer writhing off the blacktop. Dancy Flammarion is walking towards him up the entrance ramp to the interstate, a small girlshape beneath a huge, black umbrella, coming slowly, stubbornly through the heatbent summer day. A semi rushes past, roars past, and there's wind for a moment, though it isn't a cool wind. The truck rattles away and once again the only sound is the droning rise and fall of cicadas. The Bailiff finishes his Coke and tosses the empty bottle into the marsh at the side of the road; he takes a blue paisley bandanna from his back pocket and wipes the sweat from his face and bald head.

"A man needs a hat in a place like this," he says and Dancy stops a few feet from the car and watches him. She's wearing a pair of sunglasses that look like she must have found them lying by the side of the road, the left lens cracked and the bridge held together with a knotted bit of nylon fishing twine.

"You set me up," she says to him. "You set us all up, didn't you?"

"Maybe a nice straw panama hat, something to keep the sun from cooking his brains. Didn't Clark Gable wear one of those in *Gone With The Wind?*"

"Was it the bottle, or the boy?"

The Bailiff stuffs the blue bandanna back into his trouser pocket and winks at Dancy. "It was the bottle," he says. "And the boy, and some other people you best hope you never have to meet face to face."

"And the women?"

"No. It didn't really ever have anything much to do with The Ladies."

"Aramat's dead," she says and then another truck roars by, whipping the trash and grit at the side of the interstate into a whirlwind. When it's gone, Dancy wipes the dust off her clothes and "It was an accident," she says.

"Well now, that's a shame, I guess. I'd honestly hoped it wouldn't come to that," and The Bailiff shades his eyes and glances up at the sun. "But it was always only a matter of time. Some people are just too damn mean and crazy for their own good. Anyway, I imagine Biancabella can take care of things now."

"I don't understand."

"What don't you understand, Dancy Flammarion?"

"The boy. I mean, whose side are you on?"

And The Bailiff laughs softly to himself, then, and reaches for the bandanna again.

"You've got a lot to learn, child. You're a goddamn holy terror, all right, but you've got a *lot* to learn."

She stares at him silently, her eyes hidden behind the broken sunglasses, while The Bailiff blows his nose and the cicadas scream at each other.

"Can I have my duffel bag back?" she says, finally. "I left it in your car."

"Wouldn't you rather have a ride? This sun isn't good for regular folks. I hate to think what it'll do to an albino. You're starting to turn pink already."

Dancy looks at her forearm, frowns, and then looks back at The Bailiff.

"What about the others?" she asks.

The Bailiff raps his knuckles twice on the trunk. "Dead to the world," he says. "At least until sunset. And I owe you one after—"

"You don't owe me nothing," Dancy says.

"Then think of it as a temporary cease-fire. It'll be a nice change, having someone to talk to who still breathes."

Dancy stares at the Monte Carlo, at The Bailiff, and then at the endless, broiling ribbon of I-16 stretching away north and west towards Atlanta and the mountains.

"But I'm not even sure where I'm going."

"I thought that's why you have angels, to tell you these things."

"They will, eventually."

"Well, it's only a couple of hours to Macon. How's that for a start?"

In the marsh, a bird calls out, long-legged swamp bird and Dancy turns her head and watches as the egret spreads its wide, alabaster wings and flaps away across the cordgrass, something black and squirming clutched in its long beak.

"It's a start," she says, but waits until the egret is only a smudge against the bluewhite sky before she closes the umbrella and follows The Bailiff into the shade of the car.

About the Author

Caitlín R. Kiernan's first novel, *Silk*, won both the Barnes & Noble and International Horror Guild Awards for best first novel. Following the release of her second novel, *Threshold,* she has been hailed as "one of dark fiction's premiere stylists. Her poetic descriptions ring true and evoke a sense of cosmic dread to rival Lovecraft." Her short fiction has been collected in four volumes: *Candles for Elizabeth, Tales of Pain and Wonder, From Weird and Distant Shores,* and in a collaborative collection, *Wrong Things,* coauthored with Poppy Z. Brite. Kiernan is a vertebrate peleontologist, admirer of Victorian art and culture, and outspoken Luddite.